CAPTAIN

AWESOME

AND THE
ULTIMATE
SPELLING BEE

1st Prize Spelling Bee

By **STAN KIRBY**

Illustrated by
GEORGE O'CONNOR

LITTLE SIMON
New York   London   Toronto   Sydney   New Delhi

LITTLE SIMON

An imprint of Simon & Schuster Children's Publishing Division • 1230 Avenue of the Americas, New York, New York 10020 • Copyright © 2013 by Simon & Schuster, Inc. All rights reserved, including the right of reproduction in whole or in part in any form. LITTLE SIMON is a registered trademark of Simon & Schuster, Inc., and associated colophon is a trademark of Simon & Schuster, Inc. For information about special discounts for bulk purchases, please contact Simon & Schuster Special Sales at 1-866-506-1949 or business@simonandschuster.com. The Simon & Schuster Speakers Bureau can bring authors to your live event. For more information or to book an event contact the Simon & Schuster Speakers Bureau at 1-866-248-3049 or visit our website at www.simonspeakers.com. Designed by Laura Roode. Manufactured in the United States of America 0213 FFG

First Edition 10 9 8 7 6 5 4 3 2 1

Library of Congress Cataloging-in-Publication Data

Kirby, Stan. Captain Awesome and the ultimate spelling bee / by Stan Kirby ; illustrated by George O'Connor. — 1st ed. p. cm. — (Captain Awesome ; No. 7) Summary: Captain Awesome is up against Miss Stinky Pinky in the second grade spelling bee. [etc.] [1. Superheroes—Fiction. 2. Spelling bees—Fiction. 3. Schools—Fiction.] I. O'Connor, George, ill. II. Title. PZ7.K633529Cag 2013 [E]—dc23 2011046177

ISBN 978-1-4424-5158-2 (pbk)

ISBN 978-1-4424-5156-8 (hc)

ISBN 978-1-4424-5161-2 (eBook)

Table of Contents

A-*CHOOO!*
SNIFF!
SNURFFLE!

Eugene McGillicudy sat at his desk in Ms. Beasley's class and wiped his nose with a tissue. It was only ten o'clock, and he'd been sneezing all morning.

A-CHOO!

He did it again. Maybe Eugene shouldn't have moved his desk next

to the open window. But he had to.
It was the only way Eugene could
keep an eye out for evil while still
in school.

It was the kind of thing that
Super Dude did when he went
undercover in *Super Dude vs. the
Evil School* No. 2.

What's that?

You've never heard of Super Dude? Really?! How could you not know about the greatest superhero in the whole world? He's the superhero who single-handedly crushed The Crimson Crusher and still had enough time to rescue a baby ferret from an apple tree.

Eugene could tell you all about Super Dude because Eugene had read *every* *single* comic book starring the superhero. In fact, Super Dude was the reason Eugene became Captain Awesome.

MI-TEE!

With his best friend, Charlie Thomas Jones (also known as the superhero Nacho Cheese Man), and the class pet hamster, Turbo, Eugene formed the Sunnyview Superhero Squad to stop evil bad guys.

Eugene took a deep, happy breath. There was no evil outside the school window today. Then he let out a giant sneeze.

A-CHOOO!

"Dude, you've been sneezing all morning," Charlie whispered. "You okay?"

Charlie was right! Eugene *had*

been sneezing all morning and so had many of the other kids in class.

"Don't you see, Charlie?! It's all part of his evil plan!" Eugene whispered urgently.

"You're right!" Charlie gasped. Then he paused and added, "Whose evil plan?"

"Only the most evil of springtime villains!" Eugene replied. **"The Pollinator!"**

Released from the cold fingers of winter justice, the Pollinator had returned! Dressed in his protective bee suit, he was unleashing the power of uncontrollable sneezing, watery eyes, and stuffy noses!

"This is a job for Captain Awesome and Nacho Cheese Man!" Captain Awesome yelled as he looked out the window. "Get ready, Pollinator! I'm going to wipe your evil nose with the Tissue of Goodness!"

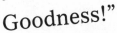

MI-TEE!

"**E** ugene . . . Eugene . . . Are you with us, Mr. McGillicudy?"

Eugene finished marking his Captain Awesome scorecard. The score was Captain Awesome 2, Pollinator 0. He closed the notebook and slid it into his desk.

"Yes, Ms. Beasley," he replied.

"It's your turn," she said.

Of course it was Eugene's turn. Isn't that always the way it works? Teachers have their own superpower. They get you right when you're thinking really important thoughts about how many times you've saved the world and crushed evil and then they ask you a question about state capitals or multiplication.

"Please come up to the board," Ms. Beasley said.

The board? Eugene swallowed hard. That was the last place any kid wanted to be: in front of the class answering a question. It was always dangerous to write on the board with all your class-mates watching your every move. Every mistake was there for the whole class to see.

I'd rather eat beets, Eugene thought.

That's when Ms. Beasley shared her plans. "I want you to spell out one of the words that will be on tomorrow's spelling test."

**GULP!
SPELLING?!
TEST?!**

Eugene shuffled his feet across the floor and made his way to the board. Charlie held out his hand as Eugene scuffed past.

"Good luck,"Charlie whispered. "You can do it, Captain Awesome!"

Eugene gave a smile. He *really* wanted to change into his Captain Awesome superhero outfit, but he was in front of the whole class!

As Eugene continued to the board, he passed by Meredith Mooney's desk. She did *not* whisper.

She liked her insults to be loud. She also liked to dress in pink from head to toe. If you poured pink lemonade into a forty-seven-inch-tall glass and floated a pink ribbon on top, you'd get the idea about just how pink Meredith looked most days.

"Dazzle us with your brains, Poo-gene," she said. "Remember, 'Duh' starts with a *capital D*." Then she stuck out her tongue.

"Meredith!" Ms. Beasley said, silencing her. "Eugene, your word is 'boat.'"

"Boat," Eugene repeated.

He looked at the board, ready to write, but his mind went blank. It was like someone had turned the lights off in his brain. He couldn't think of letters or words. His hand was frozen at his side.

Can't...move...my...arm! Eugene realized. *What kind of villain could be doing this?!*

He looked all around the room. Could it

be Meredith (aka Little Miss Stinky Pinky)? No. She was busy drawing pink unicorns in her notebook and even *she* couldn't draw unicorns *and* send a mind blast at the same time. And then Eugene saw her.

Alpha Betty!

The queen from Planet A-2-Z, evil Alpha Betty was determined to destroy all the letters of the alphabet and replace them with pictures of her evil kitty, Alpha Cat.

"She's the purrrrfect pet," Alpha Betty purred. "And instead of singing 'A-B-C-D-E-F-G . . .' everyone will be singing 'Alpha Cat, Alpha Cat, Alpha Cat, Alpha Cat, Alpha Cat, Alpha Cat, Alpha Cat . . .'"

"You'll not destroy any letters today!" Captain Awesome replied.

CHAPTER 3

First Prize?
A Hamster
Sidekick!

By
Eugene

"**B**oat." Eugene said the word again. And then once more to be sure. "Boat."

"Yes, Eugene," Ms. Beasley said. "Boat."

In *Super Dude's Springtime Annual* No. 4, Super Dude used his superboat with superstrong spray action to defeat the Water Weasel, "the world's angriest sea mammal." Thanks to Super Dude, Salty Sue and her crusty Uncle Crusty had been saved.

Eugene knew how to spell "water," but "boat" might be difficult. *I know it starts with* b, Eugene thought. *And it has to end with a* t.

And somewhere along the way there had to be an o. A *long* o. And an *a* in the middle. But in what order? Which! One! Came! First!

Eugene ran the question through his superpowered brain.

Eugene figured that since *a* is the first letter of the alphabet, it must be first. That made *o* the letter after it. He carefully wrote *b-a-o-t* under the chalk drawing of a boat on the board.

MISSION.
ACCOMPLISHED.

Eugene put the chalk down

in the tray and looked at the word again. It looked funny. Not funny like a funny joke, but funny like something was wrong with it.

And then he realized the horrible truth.

He'd spelled the word wrong.

Oh, why couldn't his word have been "captain" or "awesome"—words he could spell in his sleep? How could he get "boat" so very wrong? It only had four letters!

Eugene's heart sank into a vat of bubbling hot lava and dropped to the bottom. Or at least that's what it felt like. His stomach rumbled. He knew what was next: Meredith.

"*B-A-O-T?! What's a ba-ot?!*" Meredith exclaimed. She laughed, and several of her friends joined in as Meredith sang, "Row, row, row your ba-ot gently

down the stra-em! Merrily, merrily, merrily, merrily! Life is but a dra-em!"

Charlie wanted to change into Nacho Cheese Man and help his best friend rearrange the letters in "baot" with the help of a can of his spray cheese.

But now it was too late to fix anything.

Fortunately, Ms. Beasley, a teacher who was on the side of goodness, quieted the class. The laughter stopped. Eugene quickly erased his misspelled word and ran back to his desk.

"Okay, listen up," Ms. Beasley said. "Everyone needs to study their words tonight. Tomorrow's our weekly spelling test."

GULP.

"And I have some exciting news, class," Ms. Beasley said.

Eugene leaned forward in his seat. He didn't want to miss a single word.

"Whoever has the highest grade on tomorrow's spelling test gets a special prize," said Ms. Beasley.

Eugene loved prizes. Would it be a trip to the Sunnyview Memorial Zoo to see the elephants—Eugene's

favorite? Or a treasure chest of pirate gold? Or maybe, just maybe, pizza for lunch for a whole week?

Nope.

It wasn't any of those things. It was something better . . . and fuzzier.

"That student gets extra Turbo Time during Turbo Day tomorrow afternoon!"

EXTRA TURBO TIME!

The class erupted in cheers. The only thing better than Turbo Time was *extra* Turbo Time! Eugene thought this was better than extra TV time or extra video game time!

Turbo was the class hamster, but the fuzzy little fur ball had a secret. He was also a member of the Sunnyview Superhero Squad and

Captain Awesome's sidekick in the nonstop battle of crushing evil.

And in that battle of good vs. evil, who doesn't need the power of a superhamster?

Eugene was going to win extra Turbo Time, and no letter of the alphabet was going to stop Eugene from doing that!

CHAPTER 4

Super Tree House Study Sesh

By
Eugene

"Emergency!" Charlie called.

"*E-m-e-r-g-e-n-c-y*," spelled out Eugene. "Emergency."

"Correct!" Charlie said.

SLAP!

They high-fived.

One word down.

Twenty-four to go!

After school the boys had assembled in the Sunnyview Superhero Squad's top secret superhero base for an emergency meeting.

"By the super MI-TEE power of Captain Awesome and the canned cheese power of Nacho Cheese Man, I call this super-emergency meeting of the Sunnyview Superhero Squad to order."

Eugene took out the ceremonial Wooden Spoon of Awesomeness and banged it on the Shoebox of Justice. **WHACK!**

Today there were three items on the Squad's agenda:

1. Spelling
2. More spelling
3. Brownies

Luckily for Charlie, there was no rule that they had to be done in that order, so he stuffed a brownie into his mouth.

Spelling was important enough to list twice, but the yumminess of Mrs. McGillicudy's homemade brownies was important too. After all, superheroes have to keep up their strength with delicious snacks.

"Melling mouldn't me a mombrem!" Charlie said, his mouth full of brownie. He swallowed and tried again.

"Spelling shouldn't be a problem. We just have to keep an eye out in case Alpha Betty returns."

But Eugene knew better than to only worry about Alpha Betty. Even though spelling was one of Captain Awesome's awesome superpowers, there was always a threat to the alphabet: Little Miss Stinky Pinky.

Just like the A-B-C-Demon used his letters of destruction against Super Dude in Super Dude No. 21, Stinky Pinky would try her best to ruin tomorrow's spelling test and take the hamster prize.

The other kids didn't know

Meredith was really the bad guy Little Miss Stinky Pinky. With her pink hair ribbons, pink dress, pink socks, and pink shoes, people knew her only as the pinkest girl in all of Sunnyview. Yuck.

But to Captain Awesome and Nacho Cheese Man, Meredith was really the pinkest *villain* of all. It would be just like her to ruin the spelling test so she could hamster-nap Turbo and force him to reveal the real identities of Captain Awesome and Nacho Cheese Man.

"We've got to be ready for Little Miss Stinky Pinky too," Eugene said. "She'll try to use her brain-melting powers to melt our brains during the spelling test."

Neither one of them had forgotten that Miss Stinky Pinky had once tried to steal Turbo and smuggle him out of school in her backpack.

"She's not going to get him," Eugene vowed in his most awesome superhero voice. "I will win that extra Turbo Time."

"The only way to do that is to get the high score on Ms. Beasley's spelling test tomorrow," Charlie said.

Eugene nodded. "Score," he said. "*S-c-o* . . ." he stopped. *Wait, what was that next letter?*

"Are you ready to fail, Flunk-gene?" Meredith stood in the doorway of Ms. Beasley's classroom, filling it with her rosy awfulness.

"I'm ready to *pass* my spelling test, *My! Me! Mine! MEREDITH!*" Eugene declared. *"P-A-S-S!"*

Eugene squeezed past Meredith and plopped into his desk next to Charlie.

"You ready, Charlie?" Eugene asked.

"You bet. I brought extra cans of cheese, including the new flavor: Triple Cheddar Chili! If Little Miss Stinky Pinky tries any of her tricks, my cheese shall show no mercy!"

It's always good to have some-one watch your back with a can of superhero cheese, Eugene thought.

RING!

Everyone was in their seats and Ms. Beasley was ready with

the test. "Your first word is . . . 'boat.'" She laughed. "I want to see who was paying attention yesterday." Eugene shook his head. That was just the kind of thing a teacher would do.

The second word was "carrot." The third was "chocolate." Then "waterfall."

Ms. Beasley threw out her words to the class faster than Professor Zoom-Zoom ran circles around Super Dude in Super Dude No. 96: *The Speedster of Quickitude.*

Eugene barely had time to write down an answer before the

next word hit his ears like a dodge ball in gym class.

But if aliens ever invaded Sunnyview with a list of words to spell, Eugene would be ready. He took a deep breath and summoned all his superhero might. Ms. Beasley called out the next words.

"Railroad."

"Groceries."

"Kangaroo."

Eugene caught a glimpse of Meredith

from the corner of his eye. She was writing as fast as she could.

Then Ms. Beasley said the words that froze him in his chair, just like that time the Freezer Geezer wrapped Super Dude in a giant ice cream sandwich in Super Dude No. 48.

"*BONUS WORD.*"

A shiver ran up Eugene's back. A bonus word was one that wasn't on their study sheet. It could be any word at all.

"'Awesome,'" Ms. Beasley said.

Eugene smiled his most heroic smile. He was the first to finish. He put down his pencil with a MI-TEE *SLAP!*

Take that, Pinky, he thought as Ms. Beasley collected all the papers.

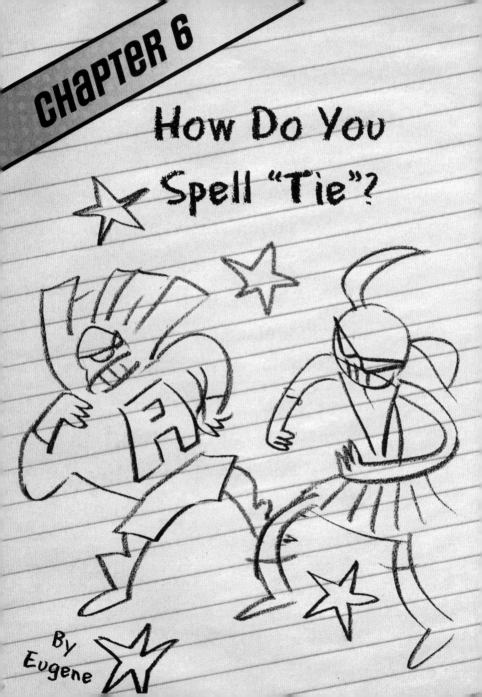

"Read quietly?" *How much longer do I have to read quietly for?* Eugene thought. It seemed to take forever plus infinity for Ms. Beasley to grade the spelling tests.

Finally she put down her red pen. "Class, I'm very pleased to announce that we have a tie for the highest grade."

Ms. Beasley pointed right at

Eugene and Meredith. "You two are tied for best speller! You'll both get extra Turbo Time today!"

GAK! thought Eugene. *Well, at least I can protect Turbo from Little Miss Stinky Pinky's evil plans!*

Mrs. Beasley continued, "I'm also excited to share that the second grade is going to have a spelling bee!"

DOUBLE GAK!

They must be called "spelling bees" because they sting when you lose, Eugene thought nervously.

"The two best spellers from

each class are going to compete for the school's spelling trophy," Ms. Beasley explained. "And I'm very happy to say that Eugene and Meredith will be representing our class!"

Eugene gasped. *Compete? In front of the school? At least Ms. Beasley's happy about it*, he thought.

But Eugene couldn't back out. There was a trophy on the line! Everyone knew that trophies weren't just a symbol of greatness. They had special trophy powers

that must only be used for good and never for evil.

This spelling bee would be the ultimate battle—not just between Eugene and Meredith, but also between Captain Awesome and Little Miss Stinky Pinky.

There could only be one winner. And it had to be Eugene. The safety of Sunnyview Elementary—and the universe—depended on it!

"I just know you'll win," Sally Williams told Eugene.

For the rest of the week Eugene spelled wherever he went.

"*B-r-o-c-c-o-l-i*," he spelled at the dinner table where his parents were used to spelling outbursts from their son. He even spelled "rutabaga," even though he was

sure that no one ever spelled it . . .
or ate it.

"*B-e-d-r-o-o-m*," he spelled in
his room, along with "blanket," "pil-
low," and "door."

"*T-o-i-l-e-t*," he spelled in the bathroom. And just to be sure, he spelled "*p-o-t-t-y*," too.

He even studied with Turbo. "*H-a-m-s-t-e-r*," he spelled, and he thought he saw Turbo give him a little nod.

SUNNYVIEW ELEMENTARY
SPELLING BEE

Eugene had spent the rest of the week s-p-e-l-l-i-n-g every word he could think of until the big day finally arrived. Eugene stood on stage in the auditorium. Unfortunately, he had to stand next to Meredith because they were from the same class.

Ms. Beasley sat in the front row with the other two spelling bee judges: the school librarian and another second grade teacher named Ms. Eckles.

Behind them sat the second-grade students who were not in the bee, and behind them sat parents and family members.

"Thank you all for coming today," Ms. Eckles announced with a smile. "I'm sure you're eager to see our little spellers give it their best shot, so let the bee begin!" she said.

The librarian looked over the top of her glasses and inspected the twelve second-graders lined up

on the stage: Jake Story, Gil Ditko, Olivia Simonson, Neal Chaykin, Howard Adams, Jane Romita, Wilma Eisner, Ellen Moore, Stan Kirby Jr., Dara Sim, Meredith Mooney, and Eugene.

They stood side by side, ready for whatever wordy words awaited to trick them with blends, short vowels, and silent *e*'s.

"When it is your turn, please step forward. I will read you a word and use it in a sentence. You will then spell the word. You will only have one chance to spell it correctly. Good luck to all of you."

And with that, The Ultimate

Spelling Bee finally began!

"Gil Ditko!" the librarian announced.

Gil stepped forward. He smiled at the librarian. She did not smile back. Spelling was very serious business. Gil adjusted his glasses.

"Your word is 'sound,'" said the librarian. "Don't make a *sound*."

Gil's lip quivered and he started to sweat. His hands nervously tapped his jeans. "Um, sound. *S-o-u-n-d*. Sound."

Gil let out a sigh and then smiled.

"Correct," said the librarian.

One by one each of the students stepped forward and was challenged by the librarian and her words of trickiness.

"Correct! Incorrect! Incorrect! Incorrect!" the librarian said. Boom! Boom! Boom! And just like that Wilma Eisner, Ellen Moore, and Neal Chaykin were out.

"Eugene McGillicudy!" the librarian called out.

GULP!

Eugene felt like his feet were made of glue and he was walking through mud. He dragged himself to the edge of the stage, his heart pounding in his chest.

I wonder if Super Dude was this nervous when he battled the Exclamation Pointer for control of Grammartopia in Super Dude No. 22, Eugene thought. He couldn't help but smile at the memory of Super Dude defeating the Pointer.

"Go, Eugene!" Charlie called

out from the audience.

"SHUSH!" cried the librarian. She raised a finger to her lips and glared at Charlie.

Oh. My. Underwear! A shocking thought suddenly hit Eugene. *Why didn't I see it before?!*

Crazy as it sounds, Eugene hadn't recognized the librarian until that moment. He had been to the library dozens of times, but today was the first time he had ever seen the librarian without a finger to her lips and saying "Shush!"

The librarian had the ability to make any student go silent with a mere glance! And if her laser stare didn't work, she'd unleash the awful fury of the Super Shush!

And now here she was, judging the spelling bee?!

Evil is full of surprises, Eugene thought.

It all made sense now. The librarian was in fact The Shusher, an evil do-badress who kept kids quiet in the library and tricked them into misspelling words!

Ms. Beasley and Ms. Eckles had no idea what evil was lurking in the chair right next to them! Eugene had to warn them! But how?!

Oh! The Sunnyview Superhero Squad Hopping Foot Code! It was his only hope! Eugene began to hop up and down on one foot.

People in the audience started to giggle.

"SHUSH!" the librarian said, sweeping her finger up to her lips. The audience instantly grew silent. Everyone knew better than to mess with The Shusher!

"Hop left twice. Small hop. Big hop. Little hop, hop, hop," Charlie said to himself as he translated Eugene's hopping code into letters. "Gfosudamuggey," Charlie read

back to himself, then smacked his forehead.

"Oh, I wish I'd paid more attention to Eugene when he explained the Sunnyview Superhero Squad Hopping Foot Code to me!" he groaned.

"Eugene? Is something wrong? Do you have to go to the bathroom?"

Ms. Beasley asked, concerned.

Eugene stopped hopping.  *Next time, I'm making sure Charlie pays more attention when I explain the Sunnyview Superhero Squad Hopping Foot Code to him!* Eugene thought.

"No, Ms. Beasley," Eugene said with a sigh. "I'm ready for my word."

"Your word is 'history,'" The Shusher read from her list.

"'History,'" Eugene repeated. He closed both eyes. "Um . . . *h-i-s-t-o-r-y*?"

Eugene opened one eye in time to see Charlie burst from his chair.

"Go, Euge—"

"SHUSH!" The Shusher hissed, cutting Charlie off midcheer.

Charlie fell back into his chair. Eugene couldn't help but smile. His

superspelling powers were working perfectly.

And his hard studying didn't
hurt either.

Howard Adams got nervous and added an extra *l* to the word "volume." He had to sit down.

Olivia Simonson spelled "chant" correctly and gave a happy squeal.

Then it was Meredith's turn. "Just watch and learn, Ew-gene." Meredith snarled at Eugene. She took her place at center stage. "Hello, my name is capital *M*

Meredith, capital *M* Mooney. I'd like to thank you all for coming to share in my victory."

"You haven't won yet, dear.

You still need to spell your words correctly," Ms. Beasley politely reminded Meredith.

"Oh, please. That's the easy part," Meredith replied.

"Meredith, your word is 'mine,'" the librarian said.

"*WHAT*? Meredith gets an easy-peasy word like 'mine?!'" Charlie whispered to Sally. "It's, like, her favorite word. Mine! Mine! Mine!"

"'Mine.' *M-i-n* . . . um, gee, what could the last letter be?" Meredith said, pretending not to know. "Oh, I don't know. Could it be . . . *e*? 'Mine.'

As in, 'The spelling bee trophy is *mine.*'" Meredith stuck her tongue out at Eugene and strolled back to her chair.

BELLS!
WHISTLES!
ALARMS!

No, not in the auditorium, but in Eugene's head. How did he not see it before?! While other students had to dodge through a maze of words with a million letters, Meredith got to spell easy words like "mine"! It could mean only one thing. . . .

The Shusher and Little Miss

Stinky Pinky were working together to make sure evil outspelled the forces of good!

Time to teach The Shusher and Little Miss Stinky Pinky a new word, Eugene thought. *And that word is . . . CAPTAIN AWESOME!* Eugene paused. *Wait. That's two words, isn't it?*

Eugene leaped from his chair and shouted, "MI-TEE!"

"**A**re you feeling all right, Eugene?" Ms. Beasley asked as she walked Eugene back to his chair on the stage. "You don't have to continue with the spelling bee if you don't want to...."

"Oh, I want to all right," Eugene said, a big smile on his face. "I know what The Shusher and Miss Stinky Pinky are up to!"

"Ew, you are such a weirdo,

Eu-germ," Meredith whispered the moment Eugene sat down.

"A weirdo for truth, justice, and no more easy-peasy words for the bad guys during the spelling bee, you mean," Eugene replied.

The next rounds of the spelling bee went by in a blur.

"Incorrect! Correct! Incorrect! Incorrect! Incorrect!" the Shusher announced. Kids were dropping

faster than candy from a piñata. Gil Ditko, out! Jane Romita, out! Dara Sim, out! Stan Kirby Jr., out!

Soon there were only four kids left: Jake Story, Olivia Simonson, Meredith, and Eugene.

Eugene was nervous—even more nervous than the time he first tried split pea soup. It felt like the butterflies in his stomach had built a ginormous roller-coaster

and were screaming in delight as they did loop after loop after loop inside his tummy.

"Jake Story!" The Shusher said. "Your word is . . . 'browse'. As in: 'The librarian decided to browse the shelves for the right book.'"

Jake ran a hand through his red hair, which was combed back over his head. "'Browse.' B-r-o-w-z-e. 'Browse'."

"Incorrect," The Shusher said. "We love you, Jakey!" Jake's

mom called out from
the audience.

The Shusher's
finger was about to
shoot up to her lips, but
she stopped midway
and lowered it slowly.

*Even a bad guy understands
it's pretty cool to let your son know
you love him*, Eugene thought.

Jake waved to his mom and
dad and went back to his seat.

Olivia Simonson was next.
She spelled the word "million"
incorrectly.

Olivia went to sit next to Jake, leaving Meredith and Eugene.

"You might as well join them, Eu-lose," Meredith said. "There's no way you can outspell me."

"You'll never beat me!" Eugene said. "Goodness must win!"

"Ha! Yeah, right. You can't even *spell* 'victory,'" Meredith snorted.

Eugene opened his mouth, but

then stopped. *I hate it when she's right,* he thought.

"Next up, Meredith Mooney!" The Shusher announced. "Your word is . . . 'victory.' 'Victory belonged to the hero.'"

"Victory. V-i-c-t-e-r-y." Meredith

yawned. "'Victory.'" She pivoted on her foot and practically skipped back to her chair. And then she heard it.

"Incorrect!" The Shusher said.

Apparently, Meredith couldn't spell "victory" *either*.

Meredith froze. She instantly spun to face the judges. "No, I can't be wrong. Check again!"

"I'm sorry, Meredith, but you spelled the word incorrectly," The Shusher explained.

"Did not!"

"Did so."

Eugene couldn't help but smile. He loved it when bad guys argued with each other.

"Meredith, we can discuss this later, but please sit down for now,"

Ms. Beasley said in a calm voice.

Meredith's face turned redder than a tomato. It was a look her mom and dad knew very well and they covered their ears, but the explosive tantrum never came.

No shouts, no screams, no stomp-
ing. Meredith smoothed her dress,
quietly sat down, and somehow
managed to not make another
sound.

Although she still looked like
she was going to explode.

"**E**ugene, if you can spell 'victory,' you will then get one last word," Ms. Eckles explained.

"Victory . . . ," Eugene repeated. He looked at his shoes. There was no way he could spell the word, but he knew someone who could!

Eugene ran off the stage.

"Yes! I win!" Meredith said, jumping to her feet and thrusting both arms in the air.

"No, you do not win," Ms. Eckles informed Meredith. "And I'm sure Eugene has a perfectly good reason for . . . Oh my. . . ."

Ms. Eckles' words trailed off. She and The Shusher both stood in stunned silence. Eugene had not returned. Instead the world's mightiest hero, Captain Awesome, had taken the stage.

"Go, Captain Awesome!" called Charlie from the audience.

The Shusher was so shocked, she didn't even shush Charlie.

Ms. Eckles and The Shusher both turned to look at Ms. Beasley. Ms. Beasley was rubbing her forehead. "I know. I know. You warned me," she said to them.

Captain Awesome took a deep breath and mustered all his spelling powers. "Victory. V-i-c-t-o-r-y," he said without stopping once to take a breath. "'Victory.'"

"Correct!"The Shusher said.

The audience cheered! Captain Awesome's spelling powers were awesome!

"Eugene,"The Shusher began.

"Captain Awesome," Captain Awesome corrected.

"*Captain*. If you spell the next word, you win the spelling bee. Are you ready?"

Captain Awesome puffed out his chest and struck a heroic spelling pose. "Do your worst!" he announced in his most heroic voice ever.

"Your word is . . . 'shush'. As in: 'Shush that silly chitter-chatter.'"

Captain Awesome didn't say a word.

Tick. Tock. Tick. Tock. The sound of the clock filled the auditorium. Parents' arms grew tired of holding out their smartphones.

Time stretched like warm taffy, but Captain Awesome would not utter a sound.

"Did you hear me, young man?" The Shusher asked, breaking the silence. "I said, 'shush.'"

"But I didn't say anything," Captain Awesome replied.

"I know," The Shusher said. "And you need to spell your word or Meredith will get a chance to spell it and win the bee."

"Okay! I'm ready! Tell me my word!" Captain Awesome announced in his very most ready-to-spell voice.

"Your word is . . . 'shush.'"

"Come on!" Captain Awesome threw his hands up. "How can I spell my word if I can't speak?"

"Why can't you speak?" The Shusher asked.

"Because you keep telling me to shush!" Captain Awesome explained.

"No, Captain, that's your *word*,"
The Shusher explained.

"What's my word?"

"'Shush!'"

"But I'm not saying anything!"

Ms. Beasley interrupted them.
"Eugene, I mean, Captain, the word
you're supposed to spell *is* 'shush.'
She's not telling you *to* shush, she's
asking you to *spell* it."

"Well, why didn't you say
so!" Captain Awesome said.

The Shusher
made a face that
Captain Awesome

thought only his mom could make.

"Shush," Captain Awesome began slowly. "*S-u-s* . . ." He paused. Something was wrong. Something was missing.

And then he remembered what Super Dude always said: "Be brave. Be strong. Help others and always do your best. If you can do those things, then you'll never truly lose."

The butterflies stopped fluttering. Captain Awesome started over. "Shush . . . *S-H-U-S-H*. 'Shush.'"

The Shusher didn't respond. Her finger gently tapped the list of spelling words. Finally she cracked a smile. "Nice job, Captain. You win the spelling bee!"

The crowd cheered! Charlie rushed onto the stage! Ms. Beasley,

Ms. Eckles, and even The Shusher clapped!

Meredith Mooney sat in her chair, arms crossed. Her face had long ago gone past tomato and was on its way to fire-truck red.

Captain Awesome had kept the spelling bee trophy from the hands of evil! There was only one word to describe this moment . . .

MI-TEE!

1st Prize
Spelling Bee

Charlie gave Eugene a high five. "That was the most awesome thing I've seen since Super Dude defeated the Warty Wicked Witch from Wonton!" Charlie cheered. "Even Queen Stinkypants was clapping for you."

Queen Stinkypants (aka Molly McGillicudy) was Eugene's little sister.

"Thanks," Eugene said proudly.

"And check out the awesome trophy I got!" But as he turned to grab the trophy, he was met with . . .

SHOCK! SURPRISE! DOUBLE SHOCK!

The trophy was gone!

He had only turned his back on the trophy long enough to high-five Charlie and it was gone?!

"Grab your cheese, Nacho Cheese Man," Captain Awesome whispered as he scanned the auditorium. "Something stinks in this auditorium, and it's not Queen Stinkypants!"

Nacho Cheese Man quickly put on his disguise and then reached into his backpack. He pulled out a fresh can of classic nacho cheese flavor. "Let's do this," he said.

"Captain Awesome! Nacho Cheese Man!" a girl's voice cried out from behind them.

It was another superhero! And she had Meredith and the spelling bee trophy! WAIT! There was another superhero in Sunnyview?! Captain Awesome and Nacho Cheese Man were speechless.

"Hello, my name is—" Captain Awesome began, but the mysterious hero cut him off.

"I know who you are, Captain Awesome. And you, too, Nacho Cheese Man. How could I not know the two greatest superheroes in Sunnyview? Besides me, of course."

The mystery hero handed the

spelling bee trophy to Captain Awesome. "I caught Little Miss Stinky Pinky trying to sneak out the side door with your trophy."

"I wasn't really taking it! I was just borrowing it! I promise! Please don't tell anyone!" Meredith pleaded.

"Captain Awesome, it's your call. . . ," the mystery hero said.

What would Super Dude do? Captain Awesome wondered. He knew the answer.

"You're free to go, Stinky Pinky," Captain Awesome began, "but you must promise to be good and—"

"Yeah, fine, be good, whatever, I promise," Meredith said as she ran to join her parents outside.

Captain Awesome sighed, then turned to the mystery hero and said, "Thank you . . ."

But she was gone.

Captain Awesome and Nacho Cheese Man ran outside the auditorium where the other students enjoyed snacks with their parents.

"Who do you think it was?" Nacho Cheese Man asked.

"Well, I know who it *wasn't*," Captain Awesome said as Meredith stuck her tongue out at him.

The two heroes had a new mystery to solve. But it would have to wait. Right now Captain Awesome had a reason to celebrate. He had won the spelling bee!

Captain Awesome and Nacho Cheese Man made their way to where their parents were waiting for them . . . and holding the biggest batch of brownies the superheroes had ever seen.

MI-TEE!

1st Pr
Spelling Bee

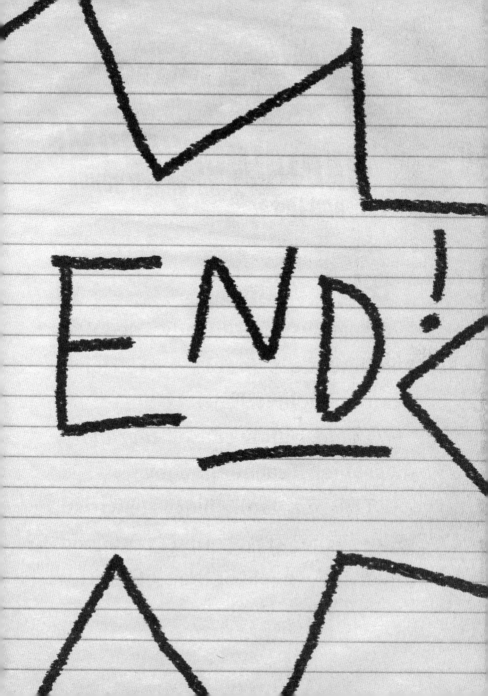

Keep reading for a sneak
peek at the next
Captain Awesome adventure!

CAPTAIN AWESOME
AND THE SPOOKY, SCARY HOUSE

"**B**oo!"

Eugene McGillicudy pedaled his bike next to his best friend, Charlie Thomas Jones.

Could Halloween be any more awesome? Eugene thought.

The dry fall leaves swirled across the street and crunched under the wheels of their bikes.

The town of Sunnyview went all out for Halloween. There were decorations in almost every yard! Houses were covered in fake spiderwebs, and pumpkins were on every porch. One yard had a mummy in a coffin, and another had Frankenstein sitting in a rocking chair. But Eugene and Charlie weren't just enjoying the spooky scenes.

They were out on patrol.

MONSTER PATROL!

MI-TEE!

Visit
CaptainAwesomeBooks.com
for completely awesome
activities, excerpts,
tips from Turbo, and
the series trailer!